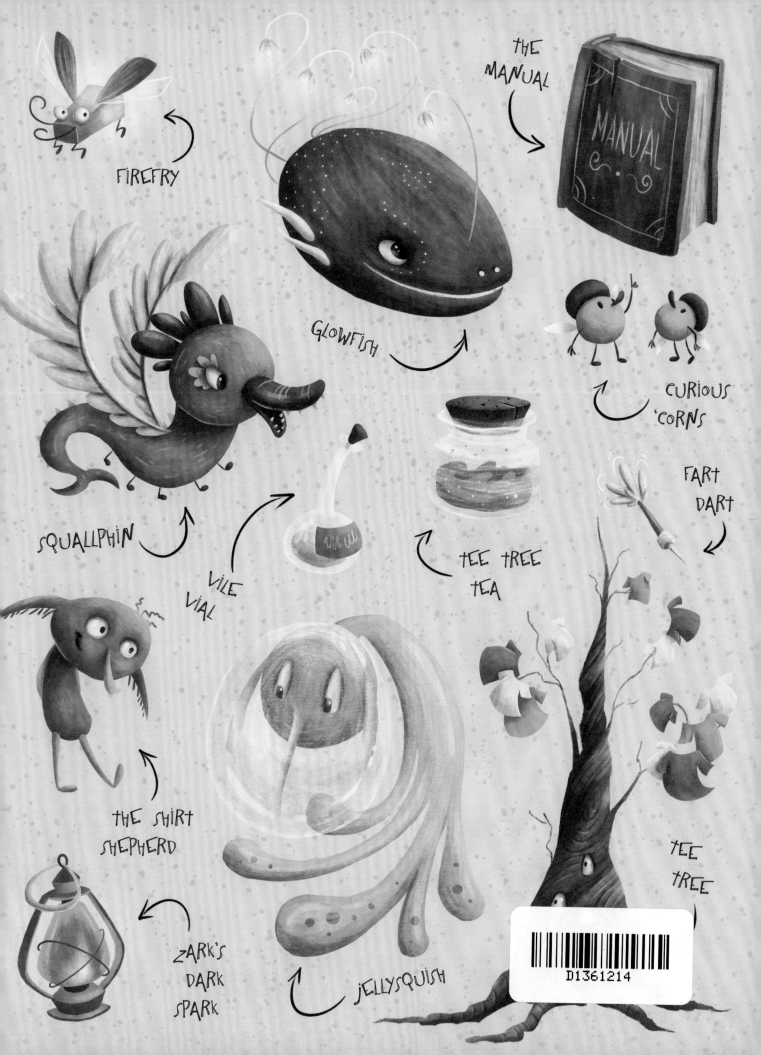

FIREFRY

THE MANUAL

MANUAL

GLOWFISH

CURIOUS 'CORNS

SQUALLPHIN

VILE VIAL

TEE TREE TEA

FART DART

THE SHIRT SHEPHERD

ZARK'S DARK SPARK

JELLYSQUISH

TEE TREE

this Book BELONGS to:

_____

_____

ZARK

• Kevin Eisenbaum •

Illustrated by
Masha Klot

PEBBLES
PRINTS

Based on the very true story
of two brave brothers.

*Special thanks to my editor and wife, Maura Eisenbaum,
and my editor and colleague, Josh Powers.*

ZARK
Text © 2020 by Kevin Eisenbaum
Illustrations © 2020 by Masha Klot
Published in the United States of America by Pebbles Prints.

ISBN 978-0-578-65446-1

The artist used digital painting and imagination to create
the illustrations for this book.
Designed by Masha Klot.

Printed and bound in China with eco-friendly soy ink.
First Edition, 2020
10 9 8 7 6 5 4 3 2 1

Explore more at
www.PlanetZark.com

FOR MY NEPHEW, JACOB,
AND YOUR ADVENTUROUS DAD.

My brother has a secret
behind his bedroom door.
He won't say what he's hiding.
He won't say what it's for.

I had to know. I *begged* to know.
"PLEEEASE tell me your secret."

But he just laughed
and shook his head.
"I don't think you can keep it."

"You're WAAAAY
too young to visit Zark.
OOPS! I've said too much...
Talk to me when you're older.
OK? Keep in touch."

I waited for my moment when he was busy watching shows,
then snuck into his room and hid beneath his filthy clothes.

I held my breath (for what must have been an hour)
and thought of how my older bro could **REALLY** use a shower.

Finally, he returned and climbed up on his bed.
"Zark needs my help again. I better go!" he said.

"Now listen
carefully."

He closed the door
to his room.
"In space you must be
brave
to avoid impending doom."

"You mean...outer space?" I said,
trying not to sound too scared.
"Should I go pack a bag or two?
I want to be prepared."

My brother sounded worried.
"This isn't a vacation.
The things we pack could save
our lives at this destination."

"Look for something useful,"
he said while crawling on the floor.
I hurried to his dresser
and opened every drawer.

I grabbed a sock. He grabbed a ball and a bear as old as he.
"Will we be gone long?" I asked. "I think I have to pee!"

"No time! We're taking off! Quick! Under the sheet!"
I jumped under the covers but forgot about my feet...

MORTAL PORTAL

"5! 4! 3!" he yelled.
"Don't let a foot get left behind!"

"2! 1! BLASTOFF!"
I pulled my feet in just in time.

The bed shook like an earthquake.
Lights shot through the dark!
Just seconds passed. The shaking stopped...

We arrived at **PLANET ZARK**.

I slowly lifted off the sheet
and could not believe my eyes.
Creatures roamed my brother's
room of every shape and size!

His bookcase rose like mountains.
His T-shirts hung like trees.
The bed dropped off like a cliff,
the floor like roaring seas.

And there he stood off
to our right
at barely two feet tall.
A spotted, plump
green fellow
with hardly any hair at all.

"I'M ZARK,"

he said with
a high-pitched voice,
a book slung at his waist.
A toothy grin above
three eyes.
He smelled like
crayons and paste.

Zark looked right at me and said,
"My friend, you really stink.
You must have brought a dirty sock,"
he added with a wink.

And while I wondered **HOW** Zark smells,
when he didn't have a nose,
my brother proudly showed him
all the items that we chose.

"You're right about the stinky sock! We also brought a ball.
And this bear named Snuggy. My friend since I could crawl."

THINGS THAT MIGHT SAVE LIVES

DIRTY SOCK

BASEBALL

SNUGGY

OTHER REALLY SUPER HELPFUL THINGS

THE MANUAL

TICKLE TICK REPELLENT

ZARK'S DARK SPARK

FOOT SHELTERS

THINGS to EAT MAYBE?

NOURISH MINTS

CANDY CRYSTALS

FIREFRIES

UNYENS

TEE TREE TEA

FUN GUYS

THINGS to AVOID!

SHADYBUGS

BARKS

BLUPS

BELLOW BOULDERS

TICKLE TICKS

CHIRPS

"Will your bear be safe?" I asked. We could have grabbed another.
He had his Snuggy way before we were even brothers!

"SHHHHH!"
Zark froze. "It's too late!
I can hear the barking now.
The Barks are here and closing in.
Listen for their growls!"

And then appeared
beyond the trees
a glow of fifty eyes.
A howl, a snarl and grinding teeth
among the yelps and cries.

"Don't move!"
Zark yelled under his breath.
"They'll see you if you do."
But my leg shook without control
as fear inside me grew.

And from the trees they emerged,
looking rather oddly.
Just heads with teeth and ears,
like dogs without a body.

The Barks grew loud
as they approached,
my heart began to pound.
My brother, acting bravely,
started running toward the sound.

He grabbed his ball from Little League
to wind up for his throw,
lifted his leg and launched the ball
as far as it could go.

The Barks stopped
right in
their tracks.

"GO FETCH!" they heard him call.
And off they raced up to the cliff
and dove after the ball.

One by one they left Zark's land. The sea washed them away.
No thanks to me and my shaky leg...my brother saved the day.

"I never should have brought you here!"

my brother yelled at me.

"How could I think you're old enough? How foolish could I be?"

"I didn't mean to shake!" I cried.
"Fine then, I'll just go!
No more Zark adventures
for your little baby bro!"

Just then a **grrrowl** made us jump, warm breath behind our backs.
One Bark still remained behind. She wanted us as snacks!

"Your bear!" Zark called. "They can't resist a fluffy toy to chew!"
My brother made a choice he hoped he'd never have to do.

He took a long look at Snuggy, his best friend from day one.
And then the Bark began to beg. Drool rolled off her tongue.

"Be good to him," my brother said. "I've always loved this bear."
The Bark was losing patience. She didn't seem to care.

And with a toss,
his bear was gone –
a goodbye to a friend.
The Bark took off into the trees
and was never seen again.

"**WAIT!**" my brother panicked, as I was no longer in sight. For the very first time today...my brother showed his fright.

He yelled my name,
his face turned white,
his eyes were open wide.
"I'm here!" I called from a distance,
running to his side.

"Where'd you go?" He sounded scared.
"Don't run away from me!"

"Just to those trees. Remember?
I REALLY had to pee."

Zark laughed. My brother smiled,
exhausted from our fight.
We grabbed Zark's tail and felt the rush
of darkness streaked with light.

Back in bed we arrived,
still covered by the sheet.
My brother's tears ran down his cheeks,
a feeling of defeat.

"I'm sorry about your bear," I sighed.
"I miss Snuggy, too."

"Don't worry," he spoke through tears.
"There was nothing you could do."

"There is one thing," I smiled. His eyes still filled with hurt.
Out came his bear that I'd been hiding underneath my shirt.

My brother let out a SQUEEEAL, relieved to see his Snuggy.
He was overwhelmed with glee. He couldn't help but hug me.

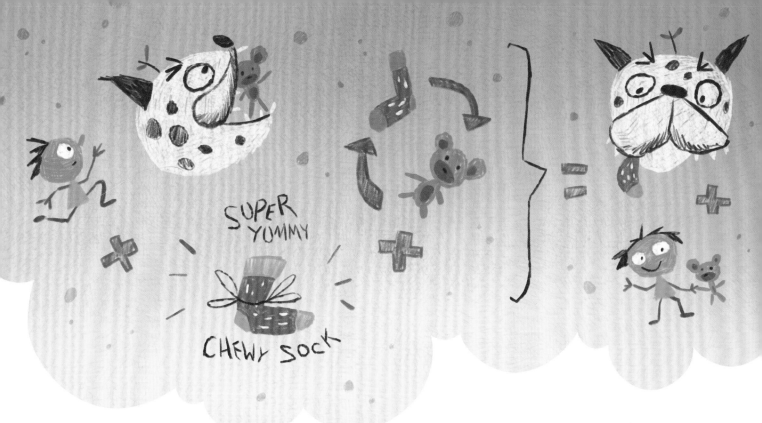

"I ran after the Bark!" I bragged. His jaw dropped in shock.
"I offered her a trade. She preferred your dirty sock."

He shook his head in disbelief.
"Well now I finally know.
I'll never visit Zark again...
without my little bro."

"Time for dinner!" Mom called,
unaware of the attacks.
And from that day on
we always knew,
we had each other's backs.

Now, my brother has a secret,
but he's not the only one.
And the **adventure** isn't over...

...it's **only** just **begun.**

BABBLE BOULDER

TONGUE TWISTERS

CHOMPY

BELLOW BOULDER

SNEEZE BALLS

SNEEZE BALL SPRAY

BAWLING BOULDER

UNYEN

BLUP

BLUP BONES

OKEYDO KEY